HOME ON THE BAYOU

a cowboy's story BY G. BRIAN KARAS

Simon & Schuster Books for Young Readers

For my family

SIMON & SCHUSTER BOOKS FOR YOUNG READERS
An imprint of Simon & Schuster Children's Publishing Division
1230 Avenue of the Americas, New York, New York 10020
Copyright © 1996 by G. Brian Karas. All rights reserved including the right of
reproduction in whole or in part in any form. SIMON & SCHUSTER BOOKS FOR
YOUNG READERS is a trademark of Simon & Schuster. Book design by Heather
Wood. The text for this book is set in New Baskerville. The illustrations are
rendered in acrylic, gouache, and pencil. Printed and bound in Hong Kong by
South China Printing Co. (1988) Ltd. 10 9 8 7 6 5 4 3 2 1 First Edition

Library of Congress Cataloging-in-Publication Data
Karas, G. Brian.
Home on the bayou: a cowboy's story / by G. Brian Karas. — 1st ed.
p.   cm.
Summary: Because he loves cowboys but can't imagine one living
in a swamp, Ned hates the move which he and his mom make to live
with Grandpa near a bayou.   ISBN 0-689-80156-4
[1. Cowboys—Fiction. 2. Bayous—Fiction. 3. Swamps—Fiction.]
I. title   PZ7.K1296Ho   1996   [E]—dc20   95-44060

Ned and his mom were moving from the West, Cowboy country, to a swamp

"Why do we have to move to a swamp?" Ned asked.
"So we can live with Granpa," said his mom.
"Is Granpa a cowboy?"
"No."
"Will there be any cowboys in the swamp?"
"I don't know, Ned."
"Why do we have to move to a swamp?"

They drove and drove.
"How about a Big Tom's Taco?" asked Ned's mom.
"How about a Big Tom's Taco?" asked Ned's mom, again.
Ned would rather eat cactus spines than answer his mom.

Ned's mom used his lasso to tie luggage to the car roof. The luggage arrived safely but his lasso did not.

"LOOK WHAT YOU DID TO MY LASSO!" screamed Ned.

"Hi, big fella," said his granpa. "Remember when I tickled your little baby toes?"

"Howdy," said Ned. "No, I don't." Ned didn't care much for Granpa's rubber boots. No decent cowboy would ever wear rubber boots.

Ned went looking for a new rope, but there were none. He made do with the garden hose. He went looking for cowboys, but there were none. "Maybe I'll find a cowboy in school tomorrow," he muttered.

"Good-bye," called his mom and
granpa.

"Good-bye, *Granpa*," said Ned. He
was mad at his mom. He tried to slam
the broken gate, but it wouldn't.

Ned counted all 957 of his steps to
school.

It looked like there was going to be a showdown before the bell rang.
Ned stared at the crowd circling around him.

"My name's Ned," he said, and he showed off his roping skills.

"Look out, here comes Big Head Ed," warned someone.

"No one calls me Big Head Ed, cowpie," and Big Head Ed gave Ned a shove. Everyone waited for Ned to lasso Big Head Ed. But Ned stood as quiet as could be. When the bell rang in the still air, they all jumped a foot.

"Later, cowpie," sneered Big Head Ed.

In class, Ned closed his eyes and thought of his old home. He saw the ridge outside his bedroom window where three giant cactus lived.

"They are the cowboys who watch over you as you sleep," his wandering daddy had told him long ago, before he wandered away. "They lasso the moon for you when it rises over their heads." Ned hoped the three cowboys watched over his daddy, wherever he might be.

". . . Ned, do you know the answer?" a voice called. It wasn't the three cowboys. It was his teacher.

"The . . . uh . . . moon?" The moon wasn't the answer.

Everyone laughed.

Ned walked home along the bayou and wondered if he could find a boat to sail west. All the boats he saw looked like they were about to sink.

"What a stupid place to live!" he said, and kicked a rock into the water. The rock stopped short of the bayou, but Ned didn't.

"WHAT A STUPID PLACE TO LIVE!!! WHY DID WE MOVE TO A SWAMP? HOW COULD YOU DO SUCH A STUPID THING?" he screamed at his mom. Then he wished he hadn't. Ned spent the rest of the day in his room, in his smelly clothes.

the next day, the Second day of School

Ned left after one spoonful of grits. "Good-bye," he said to his mom and granpa.

"Good-bye," said his granpa. His mom didn't say anything.

Ned walked to school. He practiced roping before the bell rang.

"That's not a real rope," said someone. It was the girl who sat in front of Ned. "Just watch this," he said and tried dazzling her with his technique. She wasn't dazzled. He tried some more, but she began to walk away.

"Wait . . . I can lasso the moon for you," said Ned.

"Ned is going to lasso the moon for me," she told everyone. A crowd
gathered around Ned.

"You couldn't lasso a dead alligator," said Big Head Ed.

Ned's eyes narrowed. He wanted to tie Big Head Ed to a live alligator.
A lone wind whistled through the swings. Bugs buzzed in the air.
Everyone waited for him to do something, but Ned just walked away.

No one talked to Ned that morning. No one ate lunch with him. And no one walked out with him at the end of the day.

"Don't forget that moon tomorrow, cowpie," yelled Big Head Ed.

Ned went home and waited for the moon to rise over the misty swamp. When it finally did Ned twirled his lasso and swung at the sky. It came down without the moon. He climbed a cypress tree and threw again. But his lasso landed empty, with a plop. After all of his best throwing, the moon disappeared into the mist. "YOU STUPID SWAMP!" he yelled. He pulled in his empty lasso and went to bed.

"Good-bye," said Ned's granpa. Ned walked to school slowly.

"No moon, cowpie?" asked Big Head Ed. "Don't much like your hat," he said, and threw it in the swamp. "Don't like them boots either," and he stomped on Ned's cowboy boots with his slimy shoes.

"You're a creep, Big Head Ed," said someone.

"Who said that?" Big Head Ed turned around and glared. He grabbed
Ned's lasso and twirled it in the air. "No one calls me Big Head Ed."

Big Head Ed was no cowboy. Big Head Ed was tangled up instead. Ned saw his hat sunken in the green water and looked down at his muddy boots. Then he thought he heard someone say, "Okay, Ned, it's time to do what you gotta do."

And Ned did what any decent cowboy would have done. He took the end of the hose, connected it to the faucet, and turned on the water.

The bell rang. Ned turned off the water, untied Big Head Ed, fixed a stare into his beady eyes and said, "No one calls me cowpie."

Ned was a hero. And Big Head Ed didn't show his sorry face for days.

Ned sat by the bayou gazing into the water. He straightened his hat in his reflection and there at last, but there all along, was a cowboy in the swamp.

It was Ned. He liked the way his hat looked. He liked how his boots looked new again. And he liked how he made Big Head Ed look like a big water fountain. But, he didn't like how he yelled at his mom. No decent cowboy would yell at their own mom like that. Better go do what you gotta do, he thought.

Ned went inside and gave his mom a big hug. "I'm sorry," he said.
"How sorry?" she asked.
"As sorry as this cowboy ever was in his whole life."
She hugged him back and said, "That's sorry enough for me, cowboy,"
and she gave him a brand new rope.

Ned, his mom, and his granpa had a picnic by the bayou that evening.

"Sure is a pretty night," said his mom.

"I can lasso the moon for you, Mom," said Ned.

And he did.